THE GHOST DANCE

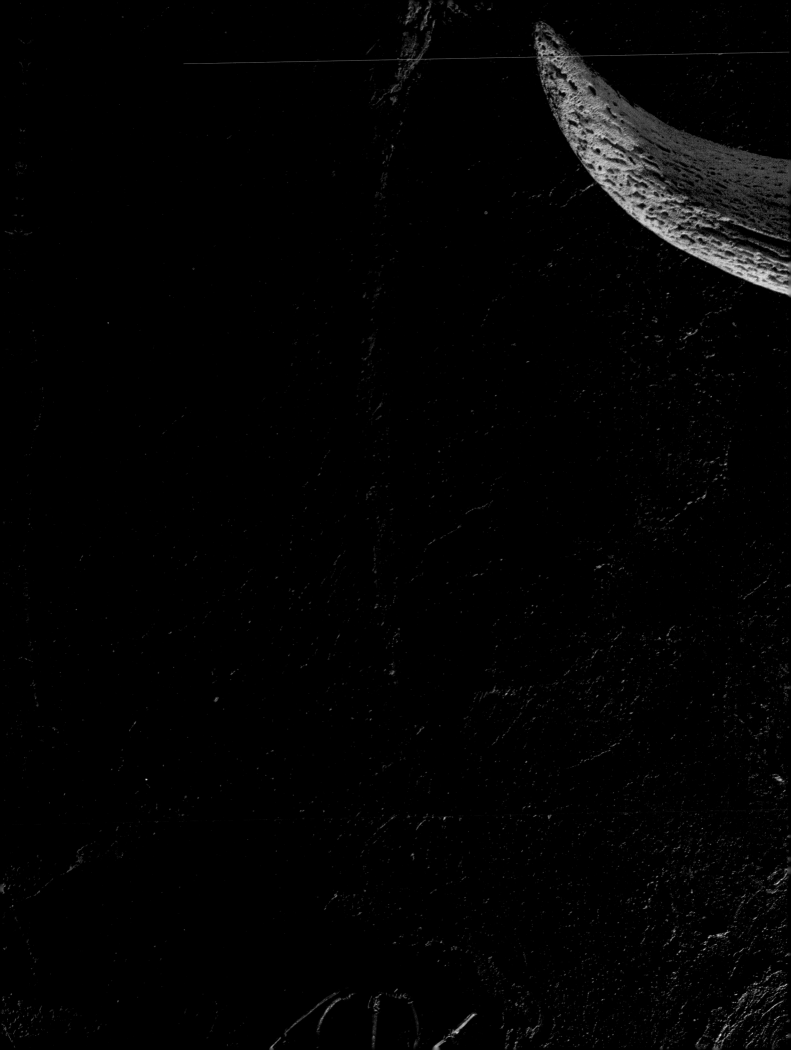

THE GHOST DANCE

By
Alice McLerran

Assemblage and paintings by
Paul Morin

Clarion Books
New York

Clarion Books • a Houghton Mifflin Company imprint • 215 Park Avenue
South, New York, NY 10003 • Text copyright © 1995 by Alice McLerran
Illustrations copyright © 1995 by Paul Morin • The text was set in
16/20-point Meridien medium • Photography by José Crespo (assemblage)
and See Spot Run. • All rights reserved • For information about permission
to reproduce selections from this book, write to Permissions, Houghton
Mifflin Company, 215 Park Avenue South, New York, NY 10003.
Printed in the USA • *Library of Congress Cataloging-in-Publication Data*
McLerran, Alice, 1933-   ISBN 0-395-63168-8   The ghost dance / by Alice
McLerran ; illustrated by Paul Morin.   p. cm.   1. Ghost dance—Juvenile
literature. 2. Indians of North America—Religion—Juvenile literature.
[1. Ghost dance. 2. Indians of North America—Religion.]   I. Morin, Paul,
1959-   ill.   II. Title.   E98.R3M35 1995   811′.54—dc20   94-34231
CIP   AC

HOR 10 9 8 7 6 5 4 3 2 1

For Narciso Lema Terán
—A. M.

To all First Nation peoples
who are rediscovering traditional ways
and spreading these teachings
—P. M.

The People lived in sunlight then.
The streams ran clear,

the wind was sweet with prairie grass,
and buffalo were many.

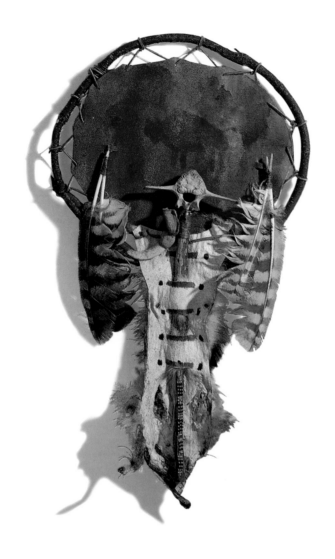

When white men came a shadow fell.
Yet with them came swift horses,
came guns more true than arrows.
Such things were surely good—
and buffalo were many.

But as more came, and more,
The People saw they wished to own the earth.
They killed the buffalo, stripped off the hides,

and left the meat to rot.
Their metal plows ripped through the prairie grass—
pushing, pushing, pushing west.

Oh, for the days of the grandfathers!
Ah, the baskets filled with pine nuts,
the fish that leaped in crystal waters,
the herds of buffalo and elk!

Ghosts now, all ghosts.

Tavibo the prophet, Tavibo of the visions—
Tavibo dreamed a dream.
Dance, said the dream.
Dance to call those ghosts alive again.
Dance, and the white men all will disappear,
their horses and their goods remain.
Dance, and the fish will fill the streams
and buffalo be many.
Dance.

Nation to Native nation, the dream raced like a flame.
The People sang the vision-song, and danced.
Dance for the ways of our grandfathers!
Dance for the lives of our children!
The white men heard,
and grew afraid.

The song was strong . . .
but bullets sang more loudly.
The magic failed.

Still, that was not to be the end.

One day the sun died in the sky
and in that darkness hope was born again.
Wovoka, he who was Tavibo's son,
to him the vision came:
the world that once was there still waited,
longing to return.
And if The People kept to peaceful ways—
doing harm to no one,
speaking only truth—
then all could dance the Ghost Dance without fear,
and make the torn earth grow new skin,
the buffalo and elk return,
and all be well at last.

So once again they danced.

The People dressed themselves in magic,
held to the dream, and danced.

But once again the magic failed, and many died.

Yet still the vision calls.
It calls each nation to the dance,
calls every voice to sing.
For on this earth all are The People, all.

If all hold to the dream, the magic will be strong—
be strong to call back what we loved the most,

and of the new keep what is good,
weave old and new in harmony.

Tavibo, Wovoka, teach us to dance!
The time has surely come.

For oh, the earth grows tired
and yet more tired.
The streams run foul,
and few birds sing.

Maybe if we all dream.
Maybe if we all sing.
Maybe if we all dance.

First in 1870 and then again in 1890, the visions of Paiute spiritual leaders sparked movements that linked native nations across two-thirds of the United States. Native Americans were seeing their lands, their peoples, their sources of food, their very cultures threatened by encroaching settlers. Eagerly they embraced the hope that by joining together in a sacred, nonviolent dance, they could restore that which had been lost. Their dream was misunderstood, and their dance mistaken for a war-dance. The tragic history of those Ghost Dance Movements of the last century ended with the massacre at Wounded Knee.

Today the sense that things are coming apart troubles nations around the globe, troubles children as well as adults. More than ever, we hunger for the very values underlying the Ghost Dance vision: a commitment to personal integrity and nonviolence, a passionate concern for social and environmental health, and a joining of purpose across political and cultural boundaries. I see the century-old Paiute vision as an oracle still offering healing. It is not a vision that failed; it is one yet to be realized.

—*Alice McLerran*

For years I've been drawn toward nature and man's connection with it. Many of the pieces I created for this book were for me an exploration of this sacred connection. Over the past year I've begun attending sweat lodge ceremonies, and this has had a great influence on me.

Throughout this book we see circles, symbolizing the "sacred hoop" of the nation, and also the cycle of seasons; the earth, moon, and sun; the circle of life. I feel that the work is both a profound personal statement and, more important, an epic universal statement.

To create the assemblage pieces, I used found and historical objects that embodied the spirit of each image: a turtle shell; hawk, crow, and eagle feathers; sage and sweetgrass; a dream catcher; wampum beads; a medicine pipe. I borrowed the ceremonial buffalo skull—it faces the sweat lodge at the western door.

In life I attempt to walk in harmony with Mother Earth, to allow some of the teachings of nature to influence my daily existence. If you touch the earth it is easy to learn respect for it.

—*Paul Morin*